For the great
Ada Madrina,
Maria Björnson

First published in 2000 by Orion Children's Books,
a division of the Orion Publishing Group,
5 Upper St Martin's Lane,
London WC2 9EA

Text and illustrations © Sally Gardner 2000
Assistant Jess Curtis

The right of Sally Gardner to be identified
as the author and illustrator of this work has been asserted.

A catalogue record for this book is available from The British Library.

Printed and bound in Italy

Dear Friends

We are thrilled to announce that due to a loophole in time we are at last able to share with the human world –

THE FAIRY CATALOGUE

So – a VERY WARM WELCOME to small people who are using *The Fairy Catalogue* for the very first time! We hope you will find it as useful as we do in Fairyland. We couldn't tell you a fairy story without it!

We believe this issue is our biggest and best so far. It gives you everything you need for your fairy tales, and MUCH, MUCH MORE.

How do we do it? We have a hundred fairies working for us! Each one is a weaver of magic and a maker of marvels. They have worked night and day to surprise and delight you.

Fairies who use this catalogue every year will know how to order, but for small people using it for the first time, here's what you do.

This catalogue is QUITE DIFFERENT from any other in your world, and this is what makes it so special: you need SEND NO MONEY!! To order any item from our treasure trove of goods, all you have to do is WISH! Because, dear children, your imagination is worth more than fairy gold.

Your dreams will be our reward.

Chief Fairy

Remember – wishes are FREE!

Orion
Children's Books

Contents

The Big Secret

IMPORTANT NOTICE

We have been producing our catalogue since once upon a time. As this is the first issue we have shared with the human world, we feel we should tell you our big secret.

It's about time.

At the very beginning of time, fairies and humans lived happily together. They played together, they had fun together. Time was a small, dull thing no human or fairy could be bothered with.

Then the great sadness of the world began. Humans began to play with time, to keep time, to beat time. And in no time at all, time became an ogre that had to be obeyed.

With time, humans grew up. With time, they grew old – too old to believe in fairies. It is the ogre time that has kept our worlds apart. This is why humans start fairy tales with *Once upon a time, a long time ago,* so that they can remind themselves of a time when time was just a small, dull thing . . .

So here's our advice to small humans using this catalogue. Remember that time doesn't matter here.

Travel freely. Travel light.

Choose Your Fairy!

We are proud to present a spectacular display of fairies –
a must for all would-be princes and princesses, and for anyone
who tells a fairy tale!

The Bad Fairy
Choose from a superb range.
Essential for any fairy story.

The Good Fairy
We bring you only the very best.
Good for party dresses, excellent for expelling wicked
stepmothers, and essential for happy endings.

The Fairy Queen
There is only one Fairy
Queen. A wish to her
could change your life.

Tooth Fairies
Think ahead! Choose a fairy you won't regret for a tooth that's loose.

The Airy Fairy
Updated to fit with modern living. Able to give you more space for your stories. A helpful friend in a tight corner.

The Cross Channel Fairy
The perfect choice for holidays, or for just popping over to France.

Water Fairies
Some have legs. Some have tails. Some are mistaken for mermaids.

The Hairy Fairy
No manners. Likes lots of noise. Very bad dress sense. A firm favourite with giants.

The Fairies at the Bottom of the Garden
There's more here than meets the eye.

Design the Perfect
Fairy Frock

All you need is your imagination! Use it to design yourself the perfect fairy frock and we will do the rest.

Blossom, dressmaker to the Fairy Queen, and her helpers Nightwing, Trip, Fancy and Pod, will work magic with needle and thimble to stitch you the dress of your dreams, made from the finest materials to be had – spider silk, thistledown, cobweb lace, waterlily silk.
OR you can go to the ball in style in one of our enchanting readymade gowns!

Choose any fabric, any colour you like.
We just give you a few ideas. The rest, my fairy friends, is up to you.

Wands, Wings and Fairy Things

What to wear with your perfect fairy frock

Wands

Is your wand spelled out? Has your magic lost its zest?
Put the sparkle back into your whizz
with one of our handmade wands.
Straight from the Grand Wizard's workshop.
In every size. Even the smallest can make
your dreams come true.

Wings

Have your wings gone floppy?
Worry not, we have wings that even butterflies envy.
Choose from our superb range of
wings that glitter,
wings that shine,
wings that make you look divine.

Fairy Shoes

Note to small people: fairy shoes are the best kept secret
in Fairyland! They help fairies fly!
Without them, we would need bigger wings.
Our shoes, handmade by elves,
are the fastest in Fairyland.
Every stitch is sealed in by
magic to give added bounce.
Choose the softest swansdown slippers,
rainbow boots or rose petal dancing shoes
to lift you off your feet.

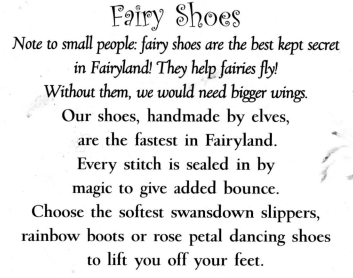

Fairy Hats

Just right for the Fairy Queen's Garden Party.

Magic Handbags

With just enough room for your wand!

Beauty Products

100 Year Night Cream

Will keep your skin looking soft and supple until your prince comes along. WE PROMISE that with our cream you won't look a day older than when you first fell asleep.

Hairy Fairy Shampoo
From the Rapunzel Collection

Goodbye to dull, listless hair, hello to the new golden you, with Rapunzel extra value shampoo! Comes in 10-gallon jars, with conditioner!

FREE and for no extra wishes, a useful booklet on what to do with ever-growing hair, including 30 different ways to plait your hair as well as a step-by-step guide to the famous ladder plait.

Here is what one satisfied customer said: *'I was locked in a tower with no means of escape. My hair was letting me down until I used Hairy Fairy Hair Products. In no time at all my hair was shining so brightly that my prince saw it and rescued me.'*

Fairy Spectacles

These rose-tinted spectacles will help you see what isn't there (or see Invisible Extras, below). If for any reason they don't work, we will send you a new pair posthaste – no questions asked!

About the quality: our spectacle frames are made out of fairy gold that comes from the heart of the magic mountain. The lenses themselves are a trade secret.

'I couldn't work without them'
Satisfied customer SALLY GARDNER

Invisible Extras

Look between this page and the next for our vast range of invisible cloaks, hats, wands etc. We regret that these goods can only be supplied to wearers of rose-tinted spectacles (see above).

Is Your Prince Charming?
Or is he just a frog?

Answer (a) (b) or (c) to each question.
The correct answers are printed below.

You are in the Royal Gardens playing with a golden ball when you see a frog sitting by the pond. Is he:

a) wearing a crown?
b) plaiting weed in his hair?
c) just plain green?

You have just lost your golden ball in the pond. Does your frog:

a) ask if he can get it back for you?
b) fetch it if you promise to give him a kiss?
c) go and hide under a lily pad?

You are having dinner with family and friends when the frog comes barging in. Does he:

a) show you up by saying you haven't kept your promise?
b) hop all over the table?
c) try to eat from everybody's plate?

Your father, the king, is not pleased to hear that you broke your promise. He insists that you keep it. Does the frog:

a) say it doesn't matter?
b) agree with your father?
c) wish he could leave the table and get back to the pond?

The frog is getting uglier by the minute. Three days have gone by and you still haven't kissed him. Does he:

a) tell you he loves you?
b) ask for a mirror to admire his own smile?
c) sit by the window and catch flies?

When you do finally kiss the frog, does he:

a) taste like old washing-up water?
b) croak loudly in your face
c) turn into the prince of your dreams?

6c, 5a, 4b, 3b, 2b, 1a

All of you with the correct answers — turn to page 6 for the dress of a lifetime!

All of you with the wrong answers – sorry! You're still at the tadpole stage.

A GREAT BARGAIN BASEMENT OFFER!

You're bound to need a family for your fairy tale, and we have searched the whole of Fairyland to bring you the very worst! All at cutdown prices ! ! !
You don't have to wish very hard to get any of them!

PLEASE NOTE: there are, of course, nice families, but what is the use of a fairy tale without a bad or hopeless father? And you can't do without a wicked stepmother. Remember – the wickeder she is, the better the happy ending!

Here is an unlucky dip of:

Dreadful dads

Missing mums

Spiteful sisters

Boorish brothers

Grumpy grannies

Cruel stepmothers

Fairy Godmother

Checklist of relatives you will need for the following fairy tales. You can order them all from *The Fairy Catalogue!*

Cinderella

Two ugly sisters, one hopeless father, one nasty stepmother, one best quality fairy godmother

Beauty and the Beast

One fond father,
two jealous stepsisters

Sleeping Beauty

One besotted mother, one doting dad, twelve doting godmothers and one wicked fairy

Hansel and Gretel

One weak dad, one evil stepmother

Twelve Dancing Princesses

One fierce father, twelve pairs of slippers
with holes in the soles

A Royal Love Story

The Bad Fairy

At Sleeping Beauty's christening, a bad fairy – who hadn't even been invited – told the king and queen that when Sleeping Beauty was sixteen she would prick her finger on a spinning wheel and die.

Complete panic broke out. The bad fairy vanished in a puff of smoke. The queen burst into tears. The king turned white. Quite a few of the courtiers fainted.

The Good Fairy

Luckily, one of the fairy godmothers still hadn't given the baby her christening present. She was only a young fairy and she hadn't got quite enough power to undo the bad fairy's magic, but she was able to change it so that the princess would not die, just fall asleep for a hundred years.

The Spinning Wheel

The king banned all the spinning wheels in the land – all but one, that stood forgotten in a turret room in a castle. On her sixteenth birthday Sleeping Beauty found it. She pricked her finger and fell fast asleep. Everyone else in the castle fell asleep too.

The Forgotten Castle

The good fairy had also put a spell on the castle, so that it would be hidden from view until a hundred years had passed. A huge forest of thorns grew up around it so that it was impossible for anyone to get through. After a few years, the castle was quite forgotten.

The Prince

Forgotten, that is, until our very own prince went out hunting and saw a ruined tower through a tangle of thorns. The thorns parted as he approached, and the prince walked up to the enchanted castle. . .

Beauty

The prince went inside. He was amazed to see the king, the queen, the courtiers, cooks, cats and dogs who had all fallen fast asleep where they stood. He went further, and found Sleeping Beauty lying on a bed of gold. He was so overcome by her loveliness that he quite forgot his manners . . .

The Kiss

and kissed her! The princess woke up. The king, queen, courtiers, cooks, cats and dogs woke up too, and went about their business as if nothing had happened. The forest of thorns vanished, and the castle stood there looking as magical as it had a hundred years ago.

The Wedding

As for the prince and princess, they decided to get married at once.

And you are invited to the wedding!

(see page 16)

Wedding Bells and Magical Spells

This is what you have all been waiting for!
We have a real treat for you – you are invited to no less
than FIVE fairy weddings! You don't have to choose one,
you can go to all of them! Just wish and you're there.
To choose your perfect outfit, turn to page 6.

The wedding dresses are designed by Blossom, the Royal Dressmaker,
and her little helpers, wonders with thimble and wand.

Cinderella's Wedding

A wedding full of enchantment, to be held in the famous glass
ballroom, with 1000 chandeliers hung from the starry night sky.
Meet the Ugly Sisters and see Cinderella's stepmother.

Sleeping Beauty's Wedding

Wake up to the perfect wedding breakfast in a castle festooned with roses and gossamer. Seven days and seven nights of festivities, including a spectacular show of fairy fireworks, attended by the Fairy Queen herself.

The Real Princess's Wedding

Very few places are available for this intimate reception to be held in the Long Room.
You are asked to wear pea-green. The bride will be holding a bouquet of sweet peas and, of course, pea soup will be on the menu. Join in the game of Hunt the Pea.

Snow White's Wedding

Held in a clearing in the forest on a snowy winter's day.
A rustic affair, laid on by seven dwarfs, who have taken endless
trouble to give Snow White the wedding of her dreams.
The trees will twinkle with diamonds and all
the animals of the forest are invited.

The Frog Prince's Wedding

A fancy dress ball in the royal gardens. Marzipan frogs and little bouncy golden balls
will be handed out to all. Boats will ferry you across the lake to an island lit up by glow worms,
where you can dance the night away to the music of the beetles.

Remember – you don't need a prince to have a wedding (though it does help).
Happy endings guaranteed!

Best Friends

Need a friend to talk to? Or a bit of that old animal magic? Then this is for you.
Get a friend – quick – before they all get snapped up!

Three Pigs

Take one or get all three.
A nicer bunch of porkers would
be hard to find. All three brothers are
in the building trade. The youngest
has just won an award for his
wolf-proof homes.

Cats

We have a wide selection of cats for
different stories. We specially recommend
Puss in Boots, the prince of cats.
A great storyteller, good at getting out of tight
corners. Has nine lives. With this cat,
you could go places!

CAUTION:
BEWARE OF CHEAP CATS PRETENDING TO BE PUSS IN BOOTS.
Ours is the only genuine one.

Golden Goose

Lays one golden egg a week.
Beware imitations – only this catalogue can
offer you the REAL golden goose!

Little Hen

Good cook, bakes her own bread, always
looking for a friend to help her.

Frogs

Worth the investment! Don't forget that one
of them could turn out to be a prince. (If not,
froggy friends can be found on pages 10 and 11)

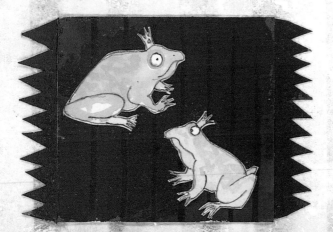

Dogs

This year, for one time only, we are
delighted to be able to offer you not just one
but THREE extraordinary dogs!

Model 1
Dog with eyes as large as teacups.
Will guard your money box.

Model 2
Dog with eyes as large as millwheels. Will
guard the family silver. Needs a lot of walks.

Model 3
Dog with eyes as large as watchtowers.
If this is the dog for you, he will guard
anything you like. WARNING: don't let him
jump up and lick your face.

Seven Dwarfs

Kind, caring and cheerful – cannot be recommended too highly! They will protect you
to the very end. You can rely on them to get rid of evil stepmothers
and keep you safe until your prince comes round.
PLEASE NOTE: cannot be supplied separately.

Unicorns

Unicorns are very rare and much wished for.
We are delighted to be able to offer you
the very best and the very last one!
Tends to be shy and doesn't like noise,
but treat it with care and you
will be well rewarded.

Friendly Giants

As regular readers of this catalogue will know,
we usually stock a large range of Friendly Giants.
Due to this year's exciting offer on dogs,
we have had to cut back on Friendly
Giants for lack of space. The Chief Fairy
would like to say sorry to any giant
who is feeling left out.

The Best of the Baddies

You'll need a few villains to liven up your fairy tale! Take your pick!

Wolves
All guaranteed to be fierce! We offer:
Wolf in sheep's clothing, wolf in Granny's nightie,
huffing and puffing wolf, wolf in cheap clothing

Foxy Fox

The well-dressed fox about the woods. Hens
and ducks should beware this dashing fellow!
He's enough to ruffle any bird's feathers.

Wicked Witches

A truly fantastic selection! Don't settle for
second worst – go for the worst, however
many wishes it costs you! All our witches can
lock princesses in towers, hand out poisoned
apples and fly on broomsticks.

Gruesome Giants

A glamorous addition to any fairy tale! Choose from: Bad-tempered giant, awesome one-eyed giant, earth-thumping giant, house-splitting giant, harp-playing ogre.

Toads

You'll need one for your witch.
CAUTION: These toads can be deadly!

Dragon

Invaluable for breathing fire into a stale tale.

Fairy Habitat

Don't delay, wish today for all the things you need for your home!

Beds

Sleeping Beauty Bed
with thornproof mattress.
100 year guarantee.

Granny Bed
perfect for receiving wolves,
woodcutters and granddaughters.

Snow White Bed
for outdoor use.
Made of glass.

Seven Dwarfs Beds
7 identical small-sized beds, very comfortable.
Available only as a set.

Beds for Bears
great big bed
for Daddy Bear,
de-luxe
middle-sized bed
for Mummy Bear,
teeny-weeny bed
for Baby Bear.

Chairs

Chairs for Bears great big chair for Daddy Bear, de-luxe middle-sized chair
for Mummy Bear, teeny-weeny chair for Baby Bear.

Magic Lamps

Complete with own genie.
Rub to make your wish come true.

Magic Mirrors

Mirror, mirror on the wall, who's the fairest
of them all? YOU ARE, of course! Wish now
and choose from our enchanting range.

Cauldrons

For cooking up spells. To make our special
fairy cakes, turn to recipe on page 26.

Spinning Wheels

For changing your future and spinning gold.
Warning: suitable for advanced storytelling only
– you can easily prick your finger. See last page
of this catalogue to undo any mistakes.

Clocks

Choose a clock that will only strike midnight –
or a clock that repeats itself – or even a clock
that makes time stand still!

Picnic Hampers

For fairy parties in forest clearings.
For food for fairy hampers see page 26.

Fairy Food

Enchanting recipes for you to make!
Magical spells to bake a cake!

Fairy Cakes

10 sugar roses
1 acorn cup of fairy dust
1 golden egg laid by a golden goose
2 acorn cups of ogre-ground flour
1 acorn cup of buttercup butter
pink pixie pods

☆ Crush the sugar roses in a bowl.

☆ Add buttercup butter and fairy dust.

☆ Whip mixture with your wand.

☆ Break the golden egg into it
and carefully add flour.

☆ Pour mixture into fairy cups,
pop pink pixie pods on top and
bake in the Seven Dwarfs' oven.

☆ When done, eat them quick
before they fly away.

Twinkle Biscuits

1 jar star beans
2 blocks of rose blossom
1 small egg laid by a little red hen
a handful of elf-raising flour
a sprinkle of fairy twinkles

☆ Beat the butter till it's barmy.

☆ Add the elf-raising flour.

☆ Ask the star beans to jump
out of the jar into the bowl
(they can be temperamental).

☆ Then add the egg and the crushed rose
blossom and stir with a runcible spoon.

☆ Put the mixture in a pat-a-cake pan,
sprinkle the twinkles on top, set your
wand to 180 degrees and wish twice.

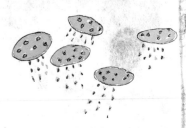

But if making half-baked cakes is all too
much like hard work, don't forget you have
a wand. With a wave and a wish the whole
cake shop could be yours.

Pumpkins and Carriages
Go anywhere and arrive in style
With our superb range of transport you can go anywhere and arrive in style.

Pumpkins
SEND NOW for a packet of pumpkin seeds PLUS a copy of *A Handy Book for Pumpkin Growers*. When pumpkin is fully grown, you can turn it into a carriage just like Cinderella's.

Broomsticks
All sorts, from the all-time classic broom to the very latest model.

Magic Carpets
The very latest in speed and comfort – came out in the 'Witch' survey with flying colours! Can take you round the world and back again.

Seven-League Boots
In seven different colours and in all shapes and sizes.

Dragonflies, Butterflies & Seahorses
We have a lovely selection!

Silver Bells and Cockleshells

Everything you need for your garden

Moon

Owing to huge demand, we are able to offer this ONCE ONLY. You will find that princes like to use it as a back-drop to that big question, 'Will you marry me?'

Starry starry sky

Goes well with moon.

Sun

Can make even the dullest tale shine bright.

Wishing Wells

A must for those who sometimes feel a little low on magic. Just fill your bucket up with wishes and your dreams will come true.

Five Magic Beans

Will grow into a giant beanstalk, or your wishes back! Packet not included. *How to use*: throw out of window. For best results: get your mother to throw the beans when she's really cross with you.

WARNING: The suppliers of the beans take no responsibility for the laying of golden eggs, or for magical harps or bad-tempered ogres. They recommend you keep an axe handy.

Barleycorn

One of our most successful items!
How to use: Plant in an old flower pot. The very next day, a flower will grow! Kiss the top of the flower. Hey presto! The petals will open and you will find a little baby girl inside.

A Packet of Peas

Find out if you are a real princess!
How to use: Place just one of our mighty green peas under 42 mattresses. Any real princess who sleeps on them will turn black and blue. Here is what one satisfied customer had to say;
'We were having so much trouble finding a real princess for our dear son. Then we tried one of your amazing peas. After only one night I was in no doubt that our son had found himself a perfect princess. We could not have wished for a happier ending.'

HEALTH WARNING:
Not to be used with fewer than 42 mattresses.
Keep out of reach of the gardener.

Nut Tree

Useless for nuts, but very good for a unique silver nutmeg and a precious golden pear. Don't ask how it's done! Following a secret recipe, our fairies have laboured long and hard, singing for centuries to perfect this little tree. We are sad to say that there is now ONLY ONE NUT TREE LEFT! All the rest seem to have been sent to the King of Spain's daughter. So order now to avoid disappointment!

Roses

The perfect gift. Use our magic

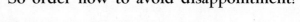

INTERFAIRY SERVICE

and send a bouquet to a princess today!

29

Dream Houses

How fantastic is your imagination? What is the home of your dreams?
Join our WISH BUILDING PLAN and you can have just what you want.
Feel free to amend and extend any of the homes listed below to suit your needs!

Shoe fits all size of family

A house that can fly away

A castle for an ogre

A tower for a princess

Tasty gingerbread house

Pumpkin – a bit of a squash

A folly for fairies

Seven Dwarfs' cottage

A secret hideaway

Granny's cottage

Toadstool house

House with ballroom

Flight of fancy

A castle for happy endings

Treetop house

31

The Fairy Bookstore

We stock a vast selection of fairy tale books.
If you want to get the background details
and find out if your favourite stories have a happy ending,
just wish for what you want. We can supply:

Beauty and the Beast • Cinderella
The Cock, the Mouse and the Little Red Hen
The Frog Prince • Hansel and Gretel
Goldilocks and the Three Bears • Jack and the Beanstalk
Jack the Giant Killer • Little Red Riding Hood
The Princess and the Pea • Puss in Boots • Rapunzel
Sleeping Beauty • Snow White and the Seven Dwarfs
The Three Little Pigs • Thumbelina • The Tinderbox
Twelve Dancing Princesses • and many more!

But remember – the fairy tales we love the best
are the ones you have made up yourself!

A Special Spell for You

Will your wishes be heard? The simple answer is yes.
We can pick up all your wishes from the smallest to the boldest.
So don't worry, just wish today and leave the rest to us.
We will not let you down. Remember, wishes are free!

We hope *The Fairy Catalogue* will make all your wishes come true.
If things get out of hand (which they easily can) don't worry –
here's a spell to make all the bad stuff go away.

Just say the upside-down word!